Lynn Downey

The Flea's Sneeze

Illustrated by

Karla Firehammer

SCHOLASTIC INC.
New York Toronto London Auckland Sydney
Mexico City New Delhi Hong Kong

ISBN 0-439-32914-0

Text copyright © 2000 by Lynn Downey.
Illustrations copyright © by Karla Firehammer.
All rights reserved. Published by Scholastic Inc., 555 Broadway, New York, NY 10012,
by arrangement with Henry Holt and Company, LLC. SCHOLASTIC and associated logos
are trademarks and/or registered trademarks of Scholastic Inc.

12 11 10 9 8 7 6 5 4 3 2 1   2 3 4 5 6/0

Printed in the U.S.A.   14

First Scholastic printing, October 2001

The artist used acrylics on Strathmore board to create the illustrations for this book.

To my husband, who always has a tissue for me

—L. D.

For Mom and Dad

—K. F.

On a dark, dark night
On an old, old farm
In a rickety, crickety
Tumbledown barn,
Everyone slept peacefully—

A rat, a cat,
A black-eyed bat;
A cow, an owl,
A feathered fowl;
A dog, a hog,
An old barn frog.

Everyone slept peacefully—
But not the flea.

No one heard him cough

"a-heh! a-heh!"

Not even the mouse
He used for a house;
Or the rat, or the cat,
Or the black-eyed bat;
Or the cow, or the owl,
Or the feathered fowl;
Or the dog, or the hog,
Or the old barn frog.

They all slept peacefully—
But not the flea.

No one heard him

"sniffle-sniffle" –

Not even the mouse
He used for a house;
Or the rat, or the cat,
Or the black-eyed bat;
Or the cow, or the owl,
Or the feathered fowl;
Or the dog, or the hog,
Or the old barn frog.

They all slept peacefully—
But not the flea.

No one heard his garbled plea,
"Does eddybody hab a tissue for be?"

Not even the mouse
He used for a house;
Or the rat, or the cat,
Or the black-eyed bat;
Or the cow, or the owl,
Or the feathered fowl;
Or the dog, or the hog,
Or the old barn frog.

They all slept peacefully—
But not the flea.

Then suddenly,
Before he could cover his snoot—

It scared the rat,
Who cried "Boohoo!"
And woke the cat,
Who hissed "Mairoo!"

Boohoo!

MairoO!

It baffled the bat,
Whose eyes turned blue,
And confused the cow,
Who muttered "Moo Moo!"

Moo
Moo!

Hoo Hoo!

It outraged the owl,
Who hollered "Hoo Hoo!"
And flustered the fowl,
Who crowed "Cock-a-doodle-doo!"
It daunted the dog,
Who barked "Woo-woooo!"
And sprayed the hog,
Who screamed "Eeeeeeww!"
And reminded the frog
Of his old nephew.

Woo-WooOO!

Cock-a-doodle-doo!

Eeeeewww!

But the mouse
The flea used for a house
Kindly gave him a tissue.

The flea wiped his nose
And before his eyes
Had even closed,
He began to doze.

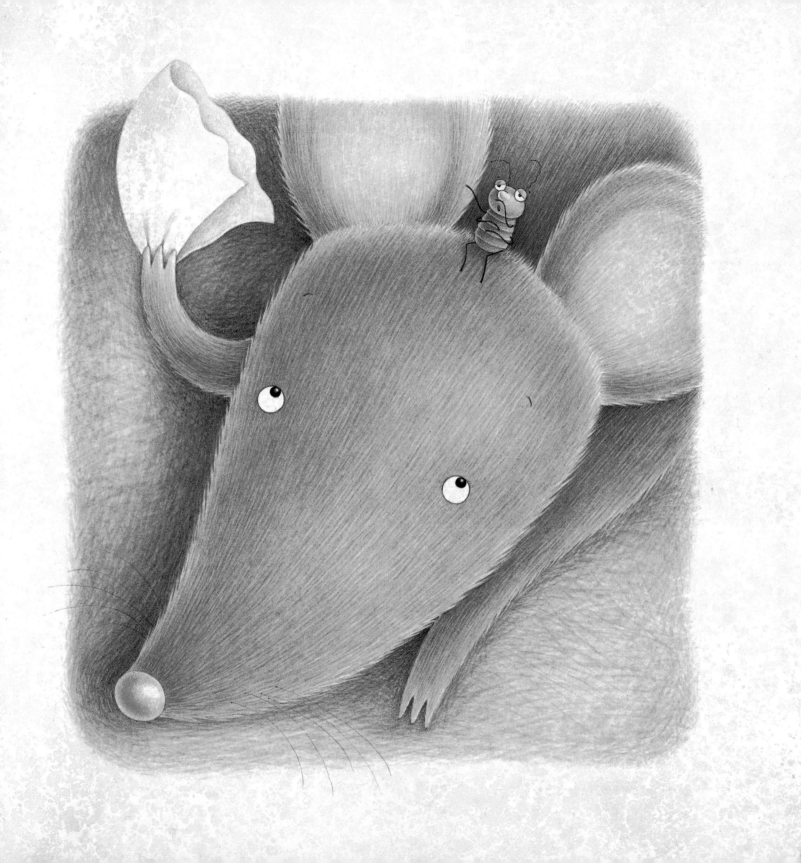

For all the rest of that
Dark, dark night
On the old, old farm
In the rickety, crickety
Tumbledown barn,
Everyone slept peacefully—

The flea and the mouse
He used for a house;
The rat, the cat,
The black-eyed bat;